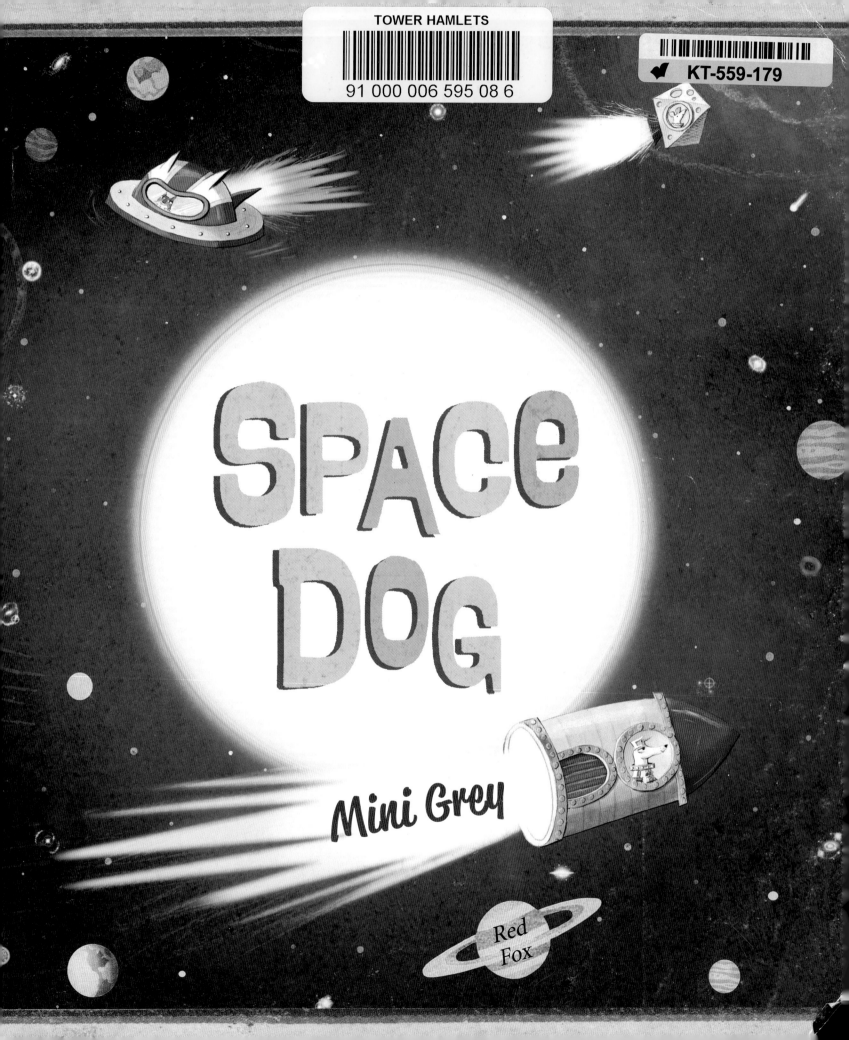

SPACE DOG

Mini Grey

Red
Fox

It's the year **3043** and, for as long as anyone can remember, on **HOME PLANET**

SPACE DOGS,

ASTRO

...have been **SWORN**

ENEMIES.

(After all, that's the way it has always been.)

But there's no time for that now, because . . .

. . . in the vast deeps of space
a small ship is zooming.

At last,
Space Dog
is about
to go

HoME

It has been a long mission sorting out planetary problems in the Dairy Quadrant.

It had all started with distress calls
from the Breakfast Cluster.

Space Dog – we need help!
Our planet is suffering
from a terrible dryness!
All our milk lakes have dried up.
We can't carry on like this.

Space Dog – we're awash with
milk, our homes are flooding –
we haven't got much time.

Sure enough, the atmosphere
on Cornflake 5 was much
too dry and crunchy . . .

. . . whereas nearby Bottleopolis
was afloat with milk.

So dry!
So dry!

Thundering
milkswamps!
I'd better hurry . . .

Aaargh, so
very dry!

It looked like a job
for Space Dog.

Things carried on . . .

with the evacuation of a Colossal Stink from Bath Time 37,

making contact with a Spaghetti Entity in the Pastaroid Belt, and rescuing the people of Niblet 12 from an escaped pet that had gone on the rampage.

Then there was just time to judge a hat competition . . .

. . . before Space Dog returned to his ship, the SS *Kennel*.

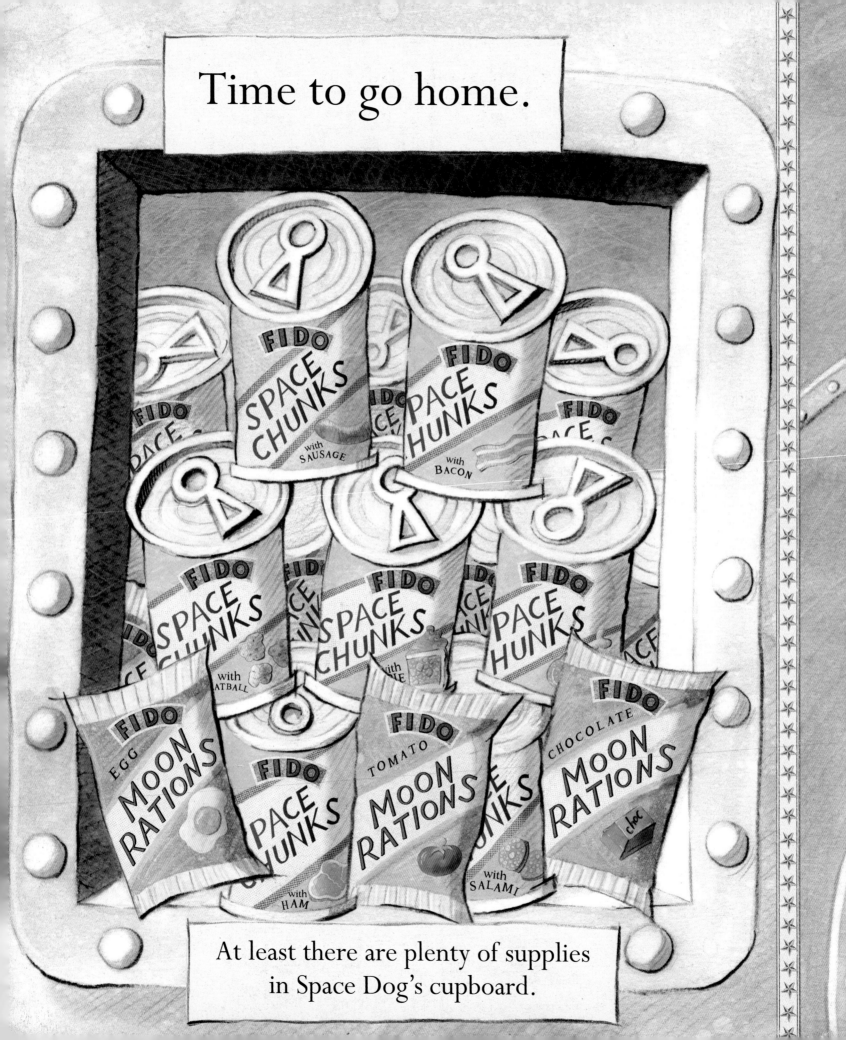

Time to go home.

At least there are plenty of supplies
in Space Dog's cupboard.

HOME SWEET HOME

No Place like Home

On board his ship
Space Dog has
his usual dinner,

* Sigh *

and then he plays
Dogopoly
on his own . . .

DOGOPOLY

Stop

GO

10

DOGOPOLY

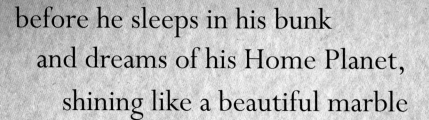

before he sleeps in his bunk
and dreams of his Home Planet,
shining like a beautiful marble
in space.

HOME PLANET

Meanwhile

somewhere not so far away in
the Dairy Quadrant, Astrocat is also
zooming in his saucer.

Mmmm, destination cream!

Suddenly Space Dog is woken by a distress call
coming through on his Laser Display Screen.

The saucer is sinking too quickly to be rescued,
but Space Dog pulls out the occupant.

AN ASTROCAT!

"But Astrocats and Space Dogs are Sworn Enemies!" gulps Astrocat.

"But there's no time for that now!" says Space Dog.

Space Dog drags Astrocat out of the thick cream and takes him aboard his own ship.

Your saucer is lost — you'd better hitch a ride in the SS *Kennel*.

GLUG

DANGER

What in CakeSpace am I going to do with an **Astrocat** on board?

When Astrocat has dried off . . .

it turns out he is surprisingly good at playing Dogopoly,

and can also rustle up a Tasty Little Something from Space Dog's supplies.

Time to **both** go home.

Space Dog and Astrocat are just setting the co-ordinates when — A DISTRESS CALL!

SOMEBODY PLEASE HELP US – THEY'RE GONNA BLOW!

Great balls of pudding! I had no idea that Astrocats could cook!

A cry for help, Astrocat.

Well, we'd better answer it then, Space Dog.

Back on the ship, Space Dog is finally setting the controls for

HOME

The UNKNOWN

when —

HOME SWEET HOME

HELP!

No Pl...

WHIFF WHIFF

SOUVENIR OF EARTH

A distress call on the Laser Display Screen! Coming from this distinctly cheesy planet. They simply **have** to help.

And look —
a Moustronaut —
tied to a skewer over
a chasm of bubbling fondue.

"Be off with you,
Cheese Ants!"
cries Space Dog.
The ants scuttle away.

"Grab my tail, Space Dog," says Astrocat,
balancing precariously and untangling the rope.

"BUT MOUSTRONAUTS AND ASTROCATS ARE SWORN ENEMIES!"
gasps the Moustronaut.
"But there's no time
for that now!"
Astrocat replies.

"MY SATCHEL!
MY SATCHEL!"
screams the
Moustronaut.

Astrocat grabs the satchel,
and, getting ready to run,
they turn round
to see . . .

Her mandibles are dribbling
and there's a hungry look
in her compound eyes.

But then
the Moustronaut
has an idea.

She offers
the Queen
the cheese
samples
from her
satchel –

Fromage

rare samples
from the farthest
reaches of space –
and bows respectfully.

The Queen
lowers her feelers.

The cheese
samples must
have been what
she wanted.
She must be a
cheese collector
too!

But this planet is full of holes and crumbling fast.

They dash to the ship and blast off just in time . . .

as, with a lurching groan, the planet implodes.

On board Space Dog's ship, they scrape the cheesy goo off the Moustronaut, and Astrocat runs her a nice bath.

But the Moustronaut has not only lost her precious cheese samples, but her Module too.

Very Important Cheese

"Cheer up, Moustronaut," says Astrocat.
"We need a quick-thinking mouse in our team.

Someone with nimble fingers

and amazing powers of sniff."

"Yes," says Space Dog.

"Someone who is brave in the face of giant insects,

and a third player for Dogopoly.

Now we can go Home."

BACK TO...
HOME PLANET — WHERE SPACE DOGS, ASTROCATS AND MOUSTRONAUTS CAN BE

ENEMIES FOR EVER

Everyone is quiet for a moment.   And then . . .

"BUT THERE'S NO TIME FOR THAT NOW!"

cries the Moustronaut.

"THERE'S A WHOLE UNIVERSE OUT THERE –

ONE WHERE SPACE DOGS, ASTROCATS AND MOUSTRONAUTS CAN BE SWORN FRIENDS."

Near to the Home button on his control panel is another one that Space Dog hasn't noticed before.

The UNKNOWN ZONE

"Shall we?"
"OF COURSE!"
"Why not!"

And they set controls for THE UNKNOWN ZONE.

In the vast deeps of space
a small ship is zooming.
Adventures could be
on the horizon,
or even just round
the corner.

But for now,
Space Dog, Astrocat and
the Moustronaut are playing
Dogopoly before dinner.

Nobody is *completely* sure
about the exact rules for Dogopoly . . .

. . . but it doesn't seem to matter.

Yoo-hoo!

Special thanks to the cosmic inspiration of Ness.

SPACE DOG
A RED FOX BOOK 978 1 849 41981 9
First published in Great Britain by Jonathan Cape,
an imprint of Random House Children's Publishers UK
A Penguin Random House Company

Penguin
Random House
UK

This edition published 2016

1 3 5 7 9 10 8 6 4 2

Copyright © Mini Grey, 2015

Red Fox books are plublished by Random House Children's Publishers UK
61–63 Uxbridge Road, London W5 5SA
www.randomhousechildrens.co.uk
www.randomhouse.co.uk

Addresses for companies within The Random House Group Limited can be found at: www.randomhouse.co.uk/offices.htm
THE RANDOM HOUSE GROUP Limited Reg. No. 954009
A CIP catalogue record for this book is available from the British Library.

Printed in China.

For
Nancy
and
Herbie